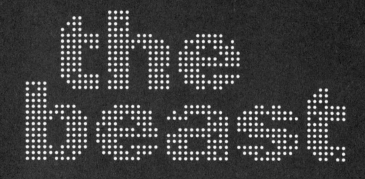

the beast

PAUL HOBLIN

darbycreek

MINNEAPOLIS

Darby Creek
A division of Lerner Publishing Group, Inc.
241 First Avenue North
Minneapolis, MN 55401 U.S.A.

Website address: www.lernerbooks.com

The images in this book are used with the permission of: Front cover: © Chris Crisman/CORBIS. iStockphoto.com/ Ermin Gutenberger, (stadium lights).

Main body text set in Janson Text 12/17.5.
Typeface provided by Adobe Systems.

Library of Congress Cataloging-in-Publications Data

Hoblin, Paul.
    The beast / by Paul Hoblin.
        p. cm. — (Counterattack)
    ISBN 978–1–4677–0301–7 (lib. bdg. : alk. paper)
    [1. Soccer—Fiction. 2. Brain—Wounds and injuries—
Fiction. 3. Sports injuries—Fiction.] I. Title.
PZ7.H653Be 2013
[Fic]—dc23   2012025222

Manufactured in the United States of America
1 – BP – 12/31/12

▦   ▦   ▦

FOR MY FRIENDS. AND, IT GOES
WITHOUT SAYING, FOR MKTK.

"a winner is that person who gets up one more time than she is knocked down."

MIA HAMM

chapter 1

As Fraser High's soccer goalie, I'm both babe and beast. Emphasis on *beast*.

I patrol the goalie box with my fangs bared. I bark orders at my teammates:

"Addie! Mark number four!"

"Olivia! Watch your left side!"

"Faith! Get back!"

It's my boyfriend, Rick Morris, who insists on adding the *babe* part. Yes, *that* Rick Morris. All-state soccer stud and all-around eye candy.

If you're wondering what Rick Morris is doing with yours truly, get in line—right behind me. When he calls me a hottie after one of my games, I wonder if my forehead is so shiny with sweat that he's actually looking at his own reflection. As far as I can tell, the only thing we have in common is that we're both goalies.

If it weren't for soccer, no one would call me a babe or a beast (at least not in a complimentary way). Instead, they'd call me bossy or even the other *b* word. Some of my teammates might call me that already. But if they do, they make sure it's said behind my back. Deep down, they know they need me.

Well, maybe not right now. During the regular season, most of our opponents are pushovers. But in a few weeks, playoffs start and we'll be up against some real competition. My teammates and our fans know that my barking might be the difference between playing in the state tournament and whatever it is that the losers do during the state tournament.

"Alyssa! Keep your head in the game!"

It's Coach Berg's voice, which is no surprise. He yells almost as much as I do. What *is* a surprise is that he's yelling at *me*. He hasn't shouted at me like this since last season.

"On the balls of your feet, Duncan!"

That's me again. Alyssa Duncan. And he's right—a goalie should never let her guard down, and I've allowed my mind to wander. Still, we're up 5–0 in the second half, and the ball's been on the other end of the field the entire game. Becca Miller, sophomore forward and rising star, scored three of those goals, using a different body part each time: the top of her foot, her head, and even her heel. Some people might consider the top of the foot and the heel to be the same body part—but those people aren't soccer players. No doubt, she'll get her picture in the local paper *again*. Not that I blame the photographer. Becca's taller than I am, but she doesn't have an ounce of beast on her body. Unlike me, she's never had to figure out whether or not being called "big-boned" is a compliment. To say she's

photogenic is an understatement. Any shot of her is a glamour shot.

"Duncan!"

What's Coach yammering about now? I realize Greenridge has invaded our half of the field. Their midfielder chips a pass over Marnie's head to a streaking forward on my left. I must not have been the only one with a brain on vacation because none of my teammates are positioned between this girl and the net.

The key to playing goalie is making quick decisions, and I do just that. The midfielder is approaching the goalie box with the ball, but she's not keeping it tight against her foot. I move forward, narrowing her angle to the net. My mind says *Now!* and I try to pounce on the ball before she has a chance to kick it. I'm a fraction of a second late. She *does* kick it, and it ricochets off my arm and away from me. I turn and lunge for the ball, but before I can grab it, I see the girl's knee coming forward. And then everything goes black.

chapter 2

hear someone say "Alyssa." Then louder: "Alyssa!" *What does he want now?*

"Duncan!"

I open my eyes. Coach Berg's face is hovering above me. So is Vicki Emmer's. She's our athletic trainer. Their faces are so bright I have to squint to see them.

"Yeah, Coach?"

"You okay, Duncan?"

He's rubbing his buzzed head, which is

what he does whenever he's mad or sad or worried or excited. I wonder what he is this time. *Mad? Sad? Worried?*

"Sure thing, Coach," I tell him. I try to sit up but can't. Vicki's holding me down with her forearm.

"Not so fast," she says and then makes a peace sign with her free hand. She asks me how many fingers she's holding up. When I tell her two, she orders me to wiggle my fingers and toes. Finally, she moves her arm and lets me sit up. A wave of wooziness nearly splashes over me again.

It's only now that I realize how confused I am. *Why is it so bright? Why are my teammates circled around me? Why am I sitting on the field?*

"Did I faint?" I wonder out loud.

"You can't remember what happened?" Vicki says.

"You had your bell rung, Duncan," Coach Berg says. He taps his temple so I know my bell is my head. "Happens to the best of us. Think you can finish the game?"

"Sure, Coach," but nodding yes sends another wave of wooziness crashing over me. I have to press my palms into the ground behind me to stay sitting up.

"There's no way you're finishing the game, Alyssa," Vicki says. She's talking to me, but her eyes are on Coach, and she looks pretty mad. "You had a concussion. We're going to get you to the hospital, okay?"

I know better than to nod my head again.

"Can your parents drive you?"

I know better than to shake my head too.

"Your dad?"

I just say "no," because it's easier than saying he died when I was two.

"Mom?"

"At work," I say.

"Well, I'm sure we can find someone who—"

"I'll do it," a voice offers.

I turn my head slowly to see that Ruth Middleton, one of our backup players, is standing next to me.

"I was thinking someone from the stands,

Ruth," Vicki says. "You're in the middle of a game."

"I don't mind," she says. Under her breath, she adds, "Don't have anything else to do."

"Coach?" Vicki says. "Can you spare Ruth for the last few minutes of the game?"

"Absolutely," he says a little too quickly. "I mean, whatever's best for Alyssa we should do, right?"

"Then it's settled," Vicki says. "Before you go, Alyssa, do you have any questions?"

Just one. "When will I get to play again?"

Vicki crouches next to me, puts my arm over her shoulder, and helps me stand up. "That's for the doctor to decide," she replies.

chapter 3

dr. Lopez is explaining my condition when a nurse pokes her head into the room and tells me I have a visitor. By the giddy way she says it, I know who's about to step into the room. Rick Morris can turn even middle-aged women into teenage admirers—especially when he's wearing a formfitting Under Armour shirt.

"Hey, babe," he says. "My club game ended early, so I stopped by your game. Everyone

told me I'd find you here."

"Here I am," I say.

"Saw Ruth in the lobby and told her I'd give you a ride home."

"Thanks."

"So this *is* the right room?" the nurse says, her eyes glued to my boyfriend's pecs. She probably expected to find a magazine model posing on the hospital bed. Instead of a beauty, she found a beast.

"Yep," I tell the nurse, "you've come to the right place." I turn to Dr. Lopez and ask, "Anything else?"

"No, I suppose not." Then she adds, "Just be careful, Alyssa. Concussions are very, very serious. Don't even think about stepping onto the soccer field until all your symptoms are gone. I want to see you again in a week, okay?"

"You're the boss," I tell her.

"Follow me, Nurse Bennett," she says on her way out. "We have other patients to check on."

Rick and I stand there looking at each other. A part of me wants to point out that he looks out of place in his workout shirt. This is

a hospital, not a sports commercial. But most of me just likes the view. And really, a torso like his deserves to be shown to the world as much as possible. Putting a regular shirt on him is like putting clothes on a famous old naked statue. It just looks wrong.

I'm thinking how fun it is to gaze at him from afar when I realize just how *far* afar is. He's still standing all the way across the room, a good fifteen feet away from me, which isn't like him at all. Usually, he can't wait to wrap his arms around me after a game.

"A concussion, huh?" he says. "At the game, they just said you got knocked out."

"I think *knocked out* and *concussion* mean the same thing, Rick."

"Really? Concussion sounds way worse."

"You know you can't catch a concussion, right?" I say.

"What do you mean?"

"I'm not contagious."

"Well, yeah," he says. "Why would you even say that?"

"Oh, no reason." Of course, there *is* a

reason. Rick's terrified he's going to get injured before he officially signs one of his Division I scholarship offers next spring.

When we first started hanging out last season, he found me sitting in my favorite tree by the soccer field and asked if he could join me. By then, I'd already spent so much time alone in that tree that I'd begun to think of it as mine. But then again, this was *the* Rick Morris, so I was happy to share with him.

Except now he won't go near the tree. Not even to touch it. I think he's worried the bark will give him a splinter that will get so infected he'll never play goalie again.

"Anyway," I tell him, "the doctor says I'll probably be able to play in a couple of weeks."

"In time for the playoffs?"

I smile. Great minds think alike. Or at least soccer players think alike. "That was the first question I asked the doctor. She thought I'd be back by then, but only if I'm feeling up for it."

"Why wouldn't you? Do you feel sick right now?"

"Just a little headache," I tell him, which is a lie. My head feels like an itty-bitty person is inside of it, trying to pound his way out with an itty-bitty sledgehammer. Everything still seems too bright. But the doctor told me these were totally normal symptoms. They'll probably go away in the next couple days—no reason to worry Rick about it. "Really, I'm sure I'll be fine in a day or two."

It's his turn to smile. He saunters over to the bed. "Good. I like you better on the soccer field than in the hospital."

I know he doesn't mean to be insensitive when he says that. I like myself better on the soccer field too.

"Two weeks, huh?" he says.

"Assuming Coach doesn't replace me with another goalie," I say.

chapter 4

'm not really worried about being replaced by another goalie. When I said it at the hospital, I meant it as a joke. After all, our backup goalie, Erin Hamley, isn't called Meat just because of her last name. It's not because she's a little on the hefty side, either. No, she's called Meat because when she's in goal, that's what she is—*dead meat.*

Coach Berg put her in several times this season when we had big leads. Every time, she

gave up goals so quickly he had to put me back in. It was our opponents who started calling her Meat—not loud enough for fans to hear but loud enough for Erin to hear. One time, Coach didn't take her out because she let in a goal. He took her out because she suddenly was crying. Between the sobs, she told us what they'd been calling her—which is when we started calling her Meat too. Not to her face and not often! But sometimes it just slips out.

It started slipping out a lot, I discovered, after the last soccer game. When I got home from the hospital, my phone was loaded with texts from my teammates. They all said pretty much the same thing.

meat gave up 3 goals in 4 minutes

meat = 3 goals for the other team

Youll never guess how many goals Meat let in . . .

I know I shouldn't admit this, but part of me *liked* getting these messages. The nickname is really mean, but this was a desperate situation. My teammates were telling me that they need me.

I stayed home from school today—doctor's orders—but decided to show up at practice to tell everyone the news. Of course, I'd already told Coach Berg I was going to miss the next couple weeks. Unlike my teammates, he didn't call me just once after the game. I must've gotten six different messages from him. "What did the doctor say?" he wanted to know. "Call me back," he pleaded. When I did, he didn't take the news well. He was so upset that he stopped talking altogether. The only noise coming from his end of the phone was the sound of him rubbing his buzzed head.

I tried to reassure him: "I should be back for playoffs, though." When he still didn't respond, I said, "Okay, Coach, I'll see you soon. Okay?" After a few more awkward silent moments, I hung up.

Again, I know it's wrong of me to think this way, but Coach's misery made me feel kinda good. He needs me, just like my teammates do, which is the biggest reason I'm on my way to practice. I can picture the scene

in my head: I arrive and all the players cheer. I announce that I'll be out for two weeks and they sob even louder than Erin Hamley.

Poor Erin, I think as I park in the athletic lot and walk to the soccer field. *There she'll be, letting shot after shot go between her legs while her teammates try to keep their voices down as they call her Meat.* I'd been so excited to be cheered for that it's only now I wonder whether I'm even supposed to be driving. The headache's still there, and so is the slight dizziness. Part of me wants to go back home and lie down, but that would mean more driving. *Besides*, I tell myself, *maybe I can give Erin some pointers on playing goalie.*

Sure, I can't teach her to be leaner or quicker. But maybe I can help her learn the basics—just to make the weeks until I return as painless as possible.

One problem: when I get to the soccer field, Erin isn't standing in front of the net. The girl who *is* patrolling the goalie box isn't short or hefty or slow. She's taller, leaner, and maybe even quicker than I am.

She's Becca Miller, our up-and-coming star forward. Or at least she *was* a forward.

The rest of the team is blasting shots at her, and she's stopping almost every one of them. One second, she's on the balls of her feet with her knees bent. The next second, she's diving to her left, her long body fully extended.

"When did you learn to play goal like this, Becca?" someone yells.

"Unbelievable, Miller—can you fly too?" adds someone else.

As I stand on the sideline, waiting for someone to notice me, I can't help thinking that Becca looks an awful lot like an up-and-coming star goalie.

chapter 5

"Duncan!"

For once, I'm glad to hear Coach Berg shout my name. It's better than listening to my teammates praise the girl who's playing *my* position.

Unfortunately, once Coach has made his way across the field to me, his voice sounds almost exactly like everybody else's. "Are you seeing this, Duncan?"

"I'm not sure. What's going . . ."

"What's going on is Becca's playing goalie."

"I can *see* that, Coach. What I'm wondering is why?"

"Why? Just take a look, Duncan. Now that you're out, I thought it might be worth switching things up a bit, so I asked Becca to give goalie a try. The girl's an absolute natural. Still rough around the edges—she doesn't know the ins and outs of goalkeeping yet—but she's got great athleticism and instincts."

Last night, Coach was so upset he couldn't talk. Now he's having trouble slowing his words to a normal human rate.

"Look at her out there, Duncan," he says, gesturing toward the field.

I had turned away from Becca to talk with Coach, but now I follow his hand back to the goal box. I hear another shout: "Watch out!"

Just then, a soccer ball shoots toward me. As I duck out of the way, another tidal wave of wooziness crashes into me and I stagger backward. Luckily, someone catches me.

"You all right?"

The voice belongs to Ruth Middleton, the girl who drove me to the hospital the day before.

"Fine," I say, hoping I sound casual enough not to worry Coach.

"Oh, my God. I'm so sorry, Alyssa."

My vision is blurry, and at first, I can't see the person who's apologizing. When my vision clears, none other than Becca Miller is standing over me. Framed by long, beautiful eyelashes, her blue eyes are showing what looks like deep concern. I feel like vomiting and not just because of the dizziness.

"I was trying to punt," Becca says, "and I've never really done that before. As you can see, I need to work on my accuracy." She smiles, and I notice her dimples for the first time. The dimples make me want to puke too.

"Like I said," I tell her, "I'm fine."

"You sure, Duncan?" It's Coach who's talking now, but if I say any more words I really am going to barf.

"I'll take her home," Ruth offers. I'd forgotten she was there, but now I realize she's

still propping me up. "Alyssa, you probably just need to lie down for a bit."

"Good idea, Middleton. Thanks for the help."

"You got it, Coach," she says. "It's the least I can do." Then she mutters, "Or maybe the *most*."

Becca says sorry one more time as Ruth drags me away from the field.

When we finally reach the parking lot, I hear Coach yelling my name one more time. "Duncan! Hold up!"

Ruth and I wait for him to catch up to us. "Yeah, Coach?" I say.

"You mind helping Becca out these next couple weeks?"

"What do you mean?"

"With her goalkeeping," he says. "Like I said, she's still a little rough around the edges. Mind smoothing her out for me? Teaching her some real technique? You know what I mean—footwork, tactics, that sort of stuff?"

I hear Ruth snicker behind me. "I guess so," I say. "I mean, yeah—of course. I'll do what I can."

"Thanks, Duncan. Oh and one more thing."

"What is it, Coach?"

"I think your yellow jersey will fit Becca better than Erin's. Make sure you get it to her before Friday's game, okay?"

chapter 6

"How you feeling?" Ruth asks me.

I'm lying in the backseat of Ruth's car as she drives me home. It's a big, old boat of a car—a Buick from way back—but I still have to bend my knees to fit in it lengthwise. My head's resting on the edge of one of the worn leather seats. Ruth adjusts the rearview mirror so she can keep an eye on me.

The combination of her question and her attentive eyes makes me think she's truly

concerned. "Pretty dizzy," I admit. "And my head is pounding."

"Sorry to hear that," she says. "But that's not what I meant. How do you feel about losing your spot?"

The comment catches me off guard. It's almost like she's reading my mind. "It's only for a couple weeks," I say weakly.

For the first time, Ruth's snicker isn't under her breath. It's so loud that it feels like it's echoing in my skull. "That's what I told myself too," she says.

"What are you talking about?"

"Did you know I used to be a starter?"

"For who?"

"For us," Ruth says. "The Copperheads."

I try to think back to a time when Ruth played in games. It's true that I just had a profound head injury, but still—I've been on varsity for two years now. You'd think I'd remember her on the field. But I don't. At all. "I thought you weren't on the team until this year."

"I actually made varsity as a freshman,"

Ruth says. That would explain why I don't remember her. She's a year older than me, so I was still playing middle school soccer when she was a freshman. "Right or left on Berkstrom Road?"

"Right," I say. I hold onto the edge of the seat as the car turns.

"After a few games, the girl ahead of me got mono, and Coach put me into the starting lineup," Ruth continues. "I did pretty well too. But then I screwed up my back and had to sit out the rest of the season. The next year I tried to come back, but Coach had already replaced me with Juanita."

"So you quit?"

"It didn't feel like I had a choice. Do I take Wilkens Avenue, or do I keep going?"

"Keep going," I say. "You were only in tenth grade. You had plenty of time to earn your way back on the field."

"That's what I told myself for a while. But it was like Coach didn't even notice me in practice, no matter how hard I worked."

"Juanita is a great player," I add. "There's

no shame in losing your spot to her."

"She's a great player *now*. But back then, before she specialized in soccer, we were about the same. I'm not trying to rag on Juanita— she's better now than I ever was, definitely. I'm just telling you how it was then."

I'm starting to feel dizzy again. "What's your point?"

"My point is, why do you think Juanita specialized in soccer? Left or right on Dobbins?"

I answer her second question—"Left"— but I can't remember the first.

Ruth goes ahead and answers it herself. "Because she wanted to keep her spot on the roster, that's why. She had to be better than all the younger players coming up."

"That's how all teams work," I say.

"No, on most teams a player just needs to be *as good as* a younger player to keep her spot. On this team, Juanita's only chance was to be better than the younger player."

Ruth asks me which way to go a few more times. Other than that, we drive in silence. My

brain feels all wobbly, and it helps to have the peace and quiet. By the time she's idling in my driveway, I've formed two questions to ask her.

The first is: "So why'd you rejoin the team this year?"

"Because screw Coach Berg," Ruth says. "He may get to decide whether I play in games, but I'm not going to let him decide whether I'm on the team."

My second question: "What are you telling me I should do?" I'm still lying on the backseat because I'm afraid that getting up will send another wave my way. I can see Ruth's eyes looking at me in the rearview mirror.

"Ask yourself whether you're better than Becca," she says.

"And if the answer's no?"

Ruth gets out of the car and walks to the back door on the other side. She opens the door and offers me her hand. "If the answer's no," she says, "come talk to me. We'll do what it takes to get your spot back."

chapter 7

When I get inside my house, I'm surprised to find my mother making spaghetti in the kitchen. A big pot of water boils on the stove as Mom places a tray of garlic bread in the oven.

"What are you doing here?" I ask.

"Well, hello to you too," she says.

"You know what I mean. Aren't you supposed to be working?"

Mom has had two jobs ever since my father

died—which is to say, for as long as I can remember. During the day, she's a secretary at a law firm. In the evening, she's a waitress at a sports bar. Or at least she *was* a waitress. "Did . . . you lose your job or something?"

"Just the opposite," she says. She hands me two napkins to place on the table. "I got a promotion. I was going to tell you last night, but you were already asleep."

I don't want to talk about last night, so I change the subject back to her. "Did Alan finally retire?" Alan's the restaurant manager.

"No, but he gave me a raise," Mom says. She hands me two forks and adds, "He also gave me Wednesdays off."

"Nice," I say and take two plates from her.

"It's better than nice, Alyssa. At last, I get to see the Fraser Copperheads' star goalie."

She's talking about me, of course, but for a split second I think she's talking about Becca Miller. Then I realize she doesn't even know who Becca is or, for that matter, why she's taking my place in front of the net. When the hospital called last night and asked to speak to

Mom, she was still at work. Rather than take a message, I told the nurse to hold on a second. Then I did my best impression of my mother's voice. I did this for my mom's sake. She can get really worked up over bad news, especially when it involves me, and I didn't want her to worry.

One time, when I was a little kid, I fell from a jungle gym and broke my pinkie. Mom cried the entire way to the emergency room. She has never forgiven herself for not doing a better job spotting me. My pinkie is still a little crooked. Every once in a while, I catch Mom looking at it and her eyes well up. Besides, the last thing I want to do is tell her that I'll be warming the bench for the foreseeable future. The only reason we're able to afford my playing soccer is because she works so much. The idea of sitting on the sidelines while she's working two jobs makes me feel really guilty.

"I checked your schedule," Mom says. "You have a game next Wednesday. Hope there's room for one more person in the stands."

She takes a noodle from the boiling pot and flings it against the wall. It sticks, which means the pasta is ready. She turns around with a huge smile, but I doubt it's because of her spaghetti success. After all the shifts she spent waiting tables, she thinks she's going to get to watch me play. I know I should tell her that she's probably wrong. I just don't want to do it tonight—not when we're having dinner together on a weekday for the first time in forever.

"See you there, Mom," I reply. *Maybe I'll sit next to you.*

chapter 3

m I better than Becca at goalie? That's
what Ruth told me to ask myself, and I
spend the next day doing exactly that. I think
about it instead of thinking about English or
history or math or science. (Although it turns
out I couldn't focus on those subjects even if
I wanted to. Whenever I watch my teachers
write something on the chalkboard, waves
of wooziness start lapping against my brain
and stomach.) I think about it while eating

Italian dunkers at lunch. I think about it while everyone else plays badminton in PE. I think about it while I sit in study hall.

I'm still thinking about it when I go to practice. Coach Berg has sent Dayton Frey, Becca, and me to work on goalkeeping fundamentals. He wants me to give Becca pointers while Dayton shoots at her.

It only takes a couple of Dayton's kicks to answer the question that's been plaguing me all day. Yes, I'm definitely a better goalie than Becca Miller. For now, anyway.

Yesterday, Coach said Becca's skills needed some fine-tuning, and he was right. Her footwork is all over the place, and so is her positioning. Her grasp on angles isn't great, either.

Of course, she's able to make up for some of her poor fundamentals because of how athletic she is—that girl has some serious range. And because of how hard she tries. After only ten minutes, she's dripping with sweat and grunting loudly. Her long legs are scuffed and grass stained. There are grass

clippings in her wavy, blonde ponytail and dirt smudges on her chin and elbows.

And she doesn't seem to mind one bit. Every time she makes a diving save, she laughs and asks Dayton, "Is that the best you got?" Every time Dayton scores on her she says, "Guess not."

She's treating this whole thing like it's a big joke, which is really obnoxious—but kind of sweet too. *How*, I begin to wonder, *could I have ever been intimidated by her?*

Becca is caught leaning the wrong way and—as Dayton's shot finds the back of the net—I tell myself that she's no threat to me at all.

Looking at me as Dayton blasts another shot her way, she asks, "Any tips for me before tomorrow's game?" Before I can reply, Becca spots the airborne ball and leaps straight up into the air. She jabs at the ball with an outstretched arm and knocks it harmlessly over the net.

What an amazing play, and it happened just as I was going to suggest a few drills that

could help her footwork. If she really wants to improve, we could set up cones so she could shuffle through them—one at center-front of the goalie box and two at the corners of the goal. She could charge to the cone in front and retreat to one of the cones in the corners. I could remind her to stay in an athletic crouch, which would keep her from crossing her feet.

But I don't help her do any of these things.

"Sorry," I tell her instead, "I can't think of anything right now."

"Okay," she says, "let me know if you do."

"You got it," I say.

What I'm really thinking is: *No way, goalie girl. If you want to improve, you're going to have to do it on your own.*

Because if Becca is not a threat to me right now, why would I help her become one?

chapter 9

Once the game starts, I can't help but feel sorry for Becca. Within the first ten minutes of the first half of the game, she's given up two goals. Coach is furious.

"Don't *lean*, Miller! Get your body in front of the ball! To your right, Miller! No, not that far!"

He doesn't stop yelling for the rest of the game. He yells at her before, during, and after an Ironwood player takes a shot on goal:

"She should never have gotten that shot off!" Moments later, he shouts at her when the ball crosses midfield: "On your toes!" He even yells, "Pay attention, Miller!" when the ball's on the other end of the field.

Becca isn't the only one Coach Berg's yelling at. But she's definitely getting it worse than anyone else. Watching her take his verbal abuse, I realize that for the first time since the concussion, I'm glad I'm not in her shoes. Yesterday, Becca was all smiles. Today, she might start sobbing on the field like Erin Hamley.

It's tough to watch Becca fumble, but not as tough as watching the soccer ball. Every time it changes its course, I feel sick to my stomach. Closing my eyes is the only thing that makes the dizziness go away, but I'm afraid to keep them shut for very long in case Coach notices. If he knew about the wooziness waves, he might think I'm not getting any better.

With a couple minutes left in the game, an Ironwood player makes a right-foot flick and

goes all Abby Wambach with it. Midair and parallel to the ground, Ironwood's forward makes an amazing header into the left corner of the net. Despite the goal, we manage to beat Ironwood 4–3. Still, Coach uses his postgame speech as another opportunity to tell Becca that she has a lot to learn—"You hear me, Miller? *A lot* to learn."

"I hear you," she tells him. She sounds as though she's on the brink of tears. Coach tells her that she better be ready to go for the game on Monday and storms out of the room.

Becca may be vying for my position, but nobody deserves to get singled out for an entire game. I feel bad enough for her that I cross the room and put my hand on her shoulder. "Look," I say, "don't worry about all that screaming Coach does—okay? Seriously, he said the same stuff to me last year. The trick is not letting him get to you."

"Sounds like a difficult trick," she says. "But thanks."

"You'll get better at it, I promise."

"I hope so."

I pat her on the shoulder one more time and leave the locker room.

She catches up to me a few minutes later as I'm heading to my car. By now, it's dark outside. The headlights of other cars sweep across my vision and cause another wave of wooziness. I stagger back a little but manage to stay upright.

"The lights are still on," Becca says, pointing to the field. "Any chance you'd be willing to do some drills with me or something?"

"I wish I could, Becca, but—"

"I'll do it."

Rick is leaning against my car, biceps bursting under his spandex sleeves.

"Really?" Becca asks. "You'd do that?"

"If you're looking for goalie guidance," he says, "I'm your man." He does a few hip thrusts. "Get it?" he says. He points to himself with his thumbs. "I'm a *guy*, and this"—hip thrusts again—"is my *dance. Guidance.*"

Becca giggles just like I giggled when Rick made the same lame joke to me last season.

chapter 10

Last year, when I made varsity as a sophomore, I was nothing like the beast that I am now. People who knew me at that time would have described me as shy and quiet. But shy and quiet is a bad combination if you want to play goal for Coach Berg. I'd been a goalie since elementary school, but Coach treated me like I'd never put on a jersey before. He spent the first part of the year hollering at me just like he hollered at Becca. Like her,

I just stood there and took it . . . until one day I didn't. I yelled back at him and told him to step off. To my surprise, he pretty much did. Not just that day but for the rest of the season.

All my life, I'd been like a wimpy, earthbound caterpillar hoping that I would someday become a beautiful butterfly. But at some point last season, I got sick of waiting and decided to become a beast instead.

To most people the transformation must have seemed sudden. Where had the quiet caterpillar gone? About the only one who wasn't surprised was Rick Morris. By then, he had been training me to play goalie every night for more than a month. We would meet on the field after practices and games, and he'd help me with my fundamentals—and my confidence. He told me to be assertive, to go with my instincts, and to control the game not only with my skill but also with my voice. When I became a beast, I was becoming what he wanted me to be all along.

Still, it wasn't until the beast in me emerged that Rick started to like me. I mean,

really like me. Even then, he took until fall to stop saying we were "hanging out" and start saying we were dating. It was probably a good thing he waited so long. I needed time to wrap my head around the notion that he might actually like me *that way*. Sometimes, I still have trouble believing it. But his attraction to me obviously has something to do with my bad, beasty self. He's never happier to see me than after my voice becomes hoarse from yelling at my teammates.

For some reason that I've never understood, he's never seemed to mind that I didn't turn into a butterfly. Then again, he didn't have a goalkeeping butterfly to compare me to . . . until now.

From where I'm parked now, I can't see the soccer field, but I might as well be able to. In my profoundly injured brain, I'm watching the two of them playing soccer under the lights. I can see Rick telling Becca to "trust your gut," an expression only guys with six-pack abs ever dare to use. I can see her giggling and getting better and giggling some more. The fact that

she's doing this while wearing my yellow goalie's jersey just makes it that much worse.

It took Rick months to fall for a beast like me—how long will it take him to fall for a butterfly like Becca? I can't let that happen. Come to think of it, I bet butterflies are a good source of protein for beasts.

chapter 11

9:46 PM
To: Ruth
From: Alyssa
want 2 get rid of becca miller. will u help me?

9:48 PM
To: Alyssa
From: Ruth
rip bm

chapter 12

The next morning, I find myself lying on the backseat of Ruth's car again. I still can't sit upright in a moving vehicle without the wooziness crashing down on me.

"We're here," Ruth announces when we get to the athletic parking lot.

"Remind me again why we're doing this?" I ask.

"You said you wanted to get rid of Becca, didn't you?"

"And this is going to do that?"

"It's worth a shot," Ruth says. She's watching me in the rearview mirror again.

"Why do we have to meet here?"

"Do you know of any other place that has inground sprinklers?"

"Couldn't we just douse her with a hose?" I imagine spraying Becca until she's flat on her back like I am now.

"The trick is to get her to quit on her own," Ruth says. "If Coach knows you tried to force her off the team, he'll probably kick you off instead."

Ruth's voice is impressively calm. From her mouth, the plan sounds totally logical. She's even tapping her fingers together like she's some evil genius.

"What time is it?" I ask.

Ruth's eyes leave the rearview mirror as she checks her watch. "Quarter to ten," she says, opening her door. "She'll be here any minute." After helping me out of the car, she asks, "You sure you have a ride home?"

"My mom's restaurant is just a few blocks

from here," I say. "She can give me a lift during one of her breaks."

Ruth wishes me good luck and gets back in the car. As she drives away, I head for the soccer field and go over the plan in my head. About an hour ago, I called Becca and volunteered to help her with her goalkeeping. When she accepted my offer, I told her to meet me at the field at ten o'clock. The key to the plan is Becca's punctuality. If she's more than a few minutes late, the sprinklers will already be running and Becca will remain dry and happy.

As for me, I have to pretend that I'm late. I'll "arrive" a few minutes after Becca is soaked and sobbing. I will tell her how sorry I am. "I had *no* idea that the sprinklers went off at 10:05 on Saturdays." This is partially true. I didn't know they went off at ten o' five until about twenty minutes ago when Ruth told me they did.

When I asked her how she knew, she said, "Are you kidding? I've been trying to pull this trick on Coach Berg for years. Only problem

is, I'm pretty sure he's the one who had the sprinklers put in in the first place."

Anyway, my job right now is to find a place where I can witness Becca's soggy-ing without detection. And I know just the spot.

chapter 13

I walk to the end of the soccer field and keep going until I reach the yellow poplar tree that stands behind it. *My* yellow poplar tree. Of course, it's not yellow yet, despite its name. Its leaves won't take on their gold color until the fall. One day they'll be the same green they've been all summer. The next, without warning, they'll be bursting with color.

That's exactly what happened last fall when Rick and I would sit up here together

and talk about soccer. Until our conversation changed just like the leaves. One minute we were discussing the two primary defenses—zone and man-to-man—and the next we were discussing the two of us.

Usually, we sat on different branches of the tree. But that night, as I stared at the field, he managed to move to my branch without me noticing. I was still looking at the field when he put his arm around my shoulder. This yellow poplar helped my relationship with Rick begin, and now it's going to help me save it.

I grab a branch and try to pull myself up, but the effort sends a wooziness wave my way. I slip sprawling to the ground. After a few minutes, I get up and try again. This time, I close my eyes as I hoist myself from one branch to another, and that helps a lot. It's a good thing I know this tree so well.

I find a leafy branch where I can see the field, but where no one standing on the field could see me. Then I wait. One minute, two minutes, three minutes. I check the clock on

my phone—9:59—then turn it to silent. I don't want a random call to give away my hiding spot.

Then, at ten on the nose, the butterfly arrives.

She must be taking my offer to help her seriously because she's wearing a full soccer getup: shirt, shoes, soccer socks, and cleats. She sets her bag on the edge of the track that encircles the field, takes out a soccer ball, and begins dribbling across the track and all the way to midfield.

Becca looks around—for me, probably—and then starts dribbling again. Only this time, it's full speed and right at the net below me.

That's when I realize she's talking to herself . . . *about* herself.

"Miller's charging with the ball!" she says. "She sidesteps a defender—only a couple seconds left in the game—fakes out another defender—five, four, three, two—and shoots." Becca blasts the ball with her right foot into the net.

"Goal!" she screams. "Miller's done it! She's won the game! Her teammates are lifting her on their shoulders!"

She sits on the ground and waves her arms. I can't help but imagine Becca being carried by all of us after scoring the game-winning goal.

"But wait," Becca says, getting up. "The referee rules that the game's not over. It's a tie, and there's no time to argue."

Once again, Becca gets the ball and races across the field. I watch her take off and dribble toward the other goal. She's doing the countdown again: "Five, four, three, two . . ." She brings her foot back and then forward.

Just as she's making contact with the ball, the inground sprinklers shoot go off. One of the sprinklers is only a few feet from her and sprays her at point-blank range. Another sprinkler head, farther away, sends an arc of water that lands on her face. I doubt she even got to see her shot hit the back of the net.

I wait for her to slump to the ground and make her own waterworks. But she doesn't slump. She doesn't sob.

Instead, she runs. First to the net to get her ball, then back across the field, once again dribbling. She isn't talking like an announcer anymore.

She's laughing. Loudly. She isn't devastated. She's delighted.

Maybe Ruth's not an evil genius after all.

I watch Becca score another goal in the net below me. Once she's retrieved the ball and started heading to the other end, I climb down the tree. To avoid the wooziness, I keep my eyes shut. Unfortunately, climbing down is a lot harder than climbing up. Fortunately, I fall only a few feet and land safely on my knees. I need to get away and regroup, but the only exit is next to the bleachers. I'm on the track when Becca spots me.

"Hey, Alyssa!" she hollers over the sound of the sprinklers. "Come join me!" Still laughing, she runs fifteen yards, dives, and slides on her stomach for another ten yards.

"You're getting the field all muddy," I say in a scolding voice, then turn my back to her and walk away.

chapter 14

keep walking the four blocks to Big's Bar and Grill. When I ask the hostess if my mother is around, she points to the back of the restaurant.

I find my mother writing down someone's order. I wait for her to finish before greeting her: "Hi. Any chance you can give me a ride home?"

She tells me she has a break coming up in a few minutes. "You want anything to eat or drink in the meantime?"

Mom's been working here so long that the manager, Alan, lets her feed me for free when I stop in. "Just lemonade," I say.

She gestures toward an open booth and goes to take care of her orders. The wall above me is covered with sports clippings from our local paper. Mom used to say that one day there'd be articles about me hanging there. For a while, I believed her. But I've been playing varsity goalie for two years now, and my mug shot hasn't made the paper even once. Rick Morris's face, on the other hand, is everywhere in this restaurant. So is Becca's, even though she's been playing varsity for less than a year.

"Here you go," Mom says. She slides the lemonade across the table.

"Thanks."

"I'll be ready in just a few more minutes."

I look at my phone. Two missed calls and one message—all from Becca. The last thing I want to do right now is hear her perfect perky voice. Maybe I should just give up now. Call Coach and give up soccer. Call Rick and give him up too. What's the point of fighting for

things when you're not good enough to have them?

No—that's not the attitude to have. I know that. The reason to fight is because it's the right thing to do. Anyway, it's the right thing for a beast to do.

So instead of calling Rick to dump myself, I call him to talk. These last few days, I've been worrying nonstop about us but haven't even told Rick I was concerned. I guess I was too afraid he'd say exactly what I suspected—that he wanted to trade in his beast for a butterfly.

But maybe I'm worrying over nothing. Maybe a conversation with him will put my fears to rest. Maybe we can talk here, in the restaurant, while munching on burgers and fries.

I listen to my phone ring. A split second later, I hear Rick's phone ringing too. I know it's his phone because he has a special ring for my calls. I'm the one who downloaded the ring, in fact. Whenever I call, his phone growls.

Ring, goes my phone.

Grrrrr! goes his phone.

Ring.

Grrrrr!

I get out of my booth and follow the growl. Sure enough, Rick's sitting in a corner of the restaurant. As always, his utensils are placed in the exact middle of the table. He started doing this about a month ago—just to be safe. That's how worried he is about getting injured before signing a scholarship. He can't eat unless all sharp objects have been moved away from the table's edge.

As always, he's busting out of his Under Armour.

"What are you doing here?" I ask.

"Oh, hey, babe," he says.

I wait for him to answer my question.

"I'm meeting somebody. What are you doing here?"

"My mom works here, remember? Who are you—"

"Hey, Alyssa!"

By now, I know that upbeat voice even

better than Coach's shouts. I pivot to my right, and then I'm face-to-face with the enemy. "What's going on here?"

Becca winces at the sharpness in my voice. "Nothing. I mean, when you left, I tried calling you, but you didn't pick up—so I called the next best person. Rick agreed to meet me here and give me more advice. You wanna join us?"

How dare this girl try to act all innocent! The dirt on her cheeks just makes her teeth look that much whiter, and my own cheeks start to burn.

I'm about to tell her, in the nastiest possible way, that the answer is *no*, I don't want to join them and watch my boyfriend put the moves on some blonde bimbo who wants to—

"There you are." It's my mom's voice. "Ready to go?" Stepping up next to me, she sees glances at the corner booth and adds, "Oh, hello, Rick."

"Hey, Mrs. Duncan."

Looking at Becca, my mother asks, "And who is this?"

This? This is the blonde, beautiful thief who's stealing my life—that's who *this* is.

"I'm Becca," she says, thrusting her hand toward my mother. "I'm filling in as keeper until your daughter can come back from her injury."

My mom is too surprised to shake Becca's hand. She still hasn't noticed Becca's hand, but she instinctually grabs mine. Tight. This is another thing my mom does when dealing with bad news. For some reason, clutching me makes her feel like she has more control over the situation. When I broke my pinkie as a kid, she actually had to sit on her hands to keep from grabbing my hand and injuring me even worse. "What happened, Alyssa?"

"Nothing, Mom." I know by now to keep my voice as casual as possible.

"It doesn't sound like nothing. It sounds like it's bad enough that you can't play."

"Can we talk about this in the car, Mom?"

"That sounds like a good idea," she says.

I look at Rick one more time before my mother drags me away. I consider announcing

at the top of my lungs that there's no way that stretchy thing he's wearing qualifies as a shirt under Big's "No shirt, no shoes, no service" policy. But right now, I don't think the head waitress is too concerned with the restaurant's rules. Judging by the way she's yanking me out the door, the only thing she cares about is getting her daughter in the car.

chapter 15

The second we are in the car, Mom says, "Explain yourself."

I tell her how I got injured and that I haven't been allowed to play since. I tell her about the dizziness and the headaches. I'm about to keep going when I'm interrupted by my mother's sobs.

"Oh, my God, Alyssa. All this time you've been feeling this way, and I didn't even know it. What kind of mother am I?"

"It's not your fault," I try to tell her, but she's crying too hard to listen.

"How could I not have known?" she says. She's blubbering so much I can hardly understand her. Her face is gushing with tears and mucus. "You've been suffering through a major head injury. And me? Totally clueless about it. I've been going about my day thinking everything is fine."

"Mom, everything *is* fine. I was just knocked out. It happens all the time—"

"Alan was just telling me about a kid who *died* from getting hit in the head with a puck. I felt sad for a grand total of five seconds and then forgot all about it. It's settled. Your mother is a horrible person."

"I didn't get hit with a puck, Mom—"

"I can't believe I let you go to sleep. You should never let someone with a head injury go to sleep. That's common knowledge. What was I thinking?"

"You didn't even know about it, Mom. And besides, the doctor said it was fine for me to slee—*ow!*" Mom's got my hand in a vise

grip again.

I think this is the worst I've ever seen her, and it's my fault. If I'd kept her informed all along, she might have been able to worry one day at a time. Instead, she's spent the last few minutes crying three days' worth of tears.

"How do you feel right now?" she asks.

If I've learned anything, I'll admit to her that I'm still suffering from dizziness and sometimes headaches. It's better to tell her now than have someone else tell her later.

"I'm fine, Mom. Really. No symptoms at all."

I guess I didn't learn anything. Either that or I'm just a chicken. I can't bear to make my mother cry any more than she already has.

"Really, Mom," I say again. "I meet with the doctor on Tuesday. That means I'll probably get to play on Wednesday. Then you'll see that I'm completely, totally fine."

It's official. I'm insane. Why would I make a promise that I'm almost for sure not going to be able to keep? But it's the only way I can think of to get her to stop crying.

And it works. Mom finally takes a couple of deep breaths and wipes away the tears with her free hand. She even releases her grip. I shake my hand to encourage circulation.

"I'm going with you to your doctor's appointment," she says and starts the car.

Great. Now I just need to convince my doctor that my injured head is completely healthy. Actually, that'll be the easy part. The hard part will be destroying Becca Miller before Wednesday's game.

I need advice from an evil genius.

chapter 16

5:02 PM
From: Alyssa
To: Ruth
mission not accomplished. any more gr8 ideas?

5:08 PM
From: Ruth
To: Alyssa
hmmmmm let me think about it

1:08 AM
From: Ruth
To: Alyssa
i know how 2 get your goalie jersey back

chapter 17

"**W**ait," I whisper to Ruth. "You meant *literally* get my jersey back? Like, steal it?"

"It'll be tough for Becca to play goalie without a jersey," she murmurs.

We're sitting in the girls' locker room before the last bell on Monday. More specifically, we're sitting in front of Becca's locker. We're almost positive we're the only ones in here, but one can never be too careful

while plotting another person's decline. And this place won't be empty for long. The Copperheads have an afternoon game today, so our teammates will be heading down here as soon as they get out of their final classes.

"How is that supposed to work?" I ask. "Do you have a lock cutter?"

"Even better," Ruth says. "I have the combination."

She actually lifts her eyebrow a couple times. She really *is* an evil genius. "How'd you manage that?" I ask.

"Because it's not her lock—it's mine. I swapped them while she was in the bathroom after PE. When she came back and found her locker closed, I think she just assumed she'd locked it herself." Ruth stands up triumphantly, spins the combination, and takes off the lock.

"Wait," I say, "if you had time to switch the locks, why didn't you take the jersey too?"

"Because," Ruth says, "this is *your* mission, not mine. If you want to get Becca off the team, you're going to have to do it yourself."

The final bell rings.

"Clock's ticking," Ruth says. She swings the locker door open. I can see the jersey, folded neatly and resting on top of Becca's sports bag.

"It *is* my jersey," I say, standing up and reaching for it. "I should be able to take it back whenever I want, right?"

"Makes sense to me," Ruth says.

chapter 18

"Alyssa!" Coach shouts.

"Yeah, Coach?"

Rubbing his buzzed head, he barks, "Where's Becca? The game's about to start!"

"I don't know, Coach."

"Well, was she in the locker room?"

"I think so."

More head rubbing. "You think so? What do you mean you think so?"

I rub my chin as though I'm thinking

about his question. "Yes, I'm almost positive she was in the locker room, Coach."

"Well, go in there and get her, would you?"

I hadn't planned on this. I wonder if I'm going to go in there and find Becca searching endlessly for something that's not there, the contents of her locker all over the floor.

"Did you hear me, Duncan? Go in there and find our goalie!"

"I'm right here, Coach."

It's Becca's voice, but it trembles more than usual. When I look at her, I see why. Her eyes are red and raw. The skin around them is puffy. She's been crying.

"Where have you been, Miller?" Coach demands. "And where's your jersey?"

She's wearing her regular home uniform—the one that's navy blue. "I can't find it, Coach."

"What do you mean you can't find it?"

"It's not in my locker. I had it in my locker, but I don't know where it went."

I do. It's in my soccer bag.

"You lost the jersey. Is that it?"

Becca is about to start crying again. I'm sure of it. When you have a mom like mine, you get to know all the signs. First, eyes begin to wobble in their sockets. Next, the eyes mist up. Then, the floodgates burst open. It's like clockwork.

Becca's eyes have gone through the first phases, and it's only a matter of time before tears start running down her face. Or so I think. Instead of crying, Becca just gulps. Then, with surprising strength, she says, "Yes, Coach. I lost the jersey."

Coach Berg is as angry as I've ever seen him. He can't even scream for once. In fact, he can barely talk. "I told you to spend the weekend getting your head right," he sputters. "But instead of being more prepared, you tell me you've lost your jersey. Do I have that right?"

Becca swallows a couple more times and nods. "I'm sorry, Coach."

"Sorry doesn't cut it, Miller. You've let me and your team down. Do you even want to play goalie?"

The right answer is clear: *Yes, Coach.*
But Becca doesn't say that. She doesn't say anything. Maybe she's too scared of what will happen if she says the wrong thing.

"Well, do you?" Coach asks again.

Finally, Becca gives the response he's been looking for. "Yes, Coach."

"And how are you going to do that without a jersey?"

"I don't know, Coach."

Coach Berg rubs his buzzed head again and walks away. When he returns a moment later, his voice is a little softer and a little calmer—but not by much. "You'll have to use Erin's jersey," he says. "It won't fit very well, but it'll have to do." Turning, he yells, "Erin, where are you?"

She runs up and says, "Right here, Coach."

"Erin, I need you to—"

Just then the buzzer sounds. It's time to start the game.

I can almost see Coach's thoughts. He wants to send Erin and Becca back to the locker room to get Erin's jersey so Becca can

wear it. But if he does that, he won't have a goalie for the start of the game.

Ruth's plan is working out so well I have to remind myself not to feel sorry for Becca.

"Hey, Coach!" a voice says. "She can use mine." The voice is coming from the bleachers—and it belongs to Rick Morris.

For once, he's wearing a real shirt—his yellow, goalie jersey—but not for long. Pulling it off in one swift motion, he says, "My traveling game's not until later tonight. Becca can wear this 'til halftime and then switch with Erin."

He balls up the jersey and throws it to Becca. The crowd cheers loudly, either for how nice Rick is or for the surprise muscle show.

"Well, what are you waiting for, Miller?" Coach says. "Get that jersey on and get out there."

chapter 19

It's official. Becca Miller won't get out of the way. Not out of the goalie's box and not out of my boyfriend's sights.

We're playing Greenridge again, and they still stink. Becca only has to make a few plays during the whole first half, but she looks good making them. One time she has to come off the line, and she goes all out.

"Keeper!" she shouts, then smothers the ball under her body.

Another time, when Greenridge crosses the ball, Becca covers the length of the goal in a couple of long strides. Unlike the last game, she stays on the balls of her feet, shading opponents one way or the other. Good goalkeeping is a beautiful thing, and Becca definitely looks beautiful.

Of course, let's be honest—she'd look good even if she played horribly. Just ask Rick, who spends the whole first half cheering for her.

During halftime, Becca changes into Erin Hamley's jersey. Becca is taller than Erin. I knew the jersey wouldn't fit Becca's long, slender body as well as it should. As we wait for her to return from the locker room, I think that maybe, for once in Becca's beautiful life, she won't look absolutely perfect.

I should have known better.

The shorter shirt is that much more formfitting. It almost looks as if Becca's wearing her own Under Armour.

We win the game 4–1, making the jersey drama seem, within a few moments, like a distant memory. But for me, the only thing

that made the game bearable was that I had closed my eyes for most of it.

chapter 20

8:46 PM
From: Ruth
To: Alyssa
got another plan

8:52 PM
From: Alyssa
To: Ruth
4get it. i give up.

chapter 21

"So you're not feeling any symptoms at all, Alyssa?" the doctor asks.

I look at my mother, who has a vise grip on my hand. "None, Doc."

"No dizziness?"

Somehow Mom manages to squeeze my hand even harder. "Nope," I lie.

"Blurred vision?"

My hand is going to go numb pretty soon from lack of blood flow. "Nope," I lie again, "I

can see as well as ever."

"Headaches?"

Concern flashes across my mom's eyes.
"No," I reply, trying to ignore the small man
banging away with a sledgehammer inside my
head. "No headaches either."

Mom and I continue to hold hands as the
doctor studies my file and then closes it.

"Well," she says, "it seems awfully quick
for you to return to the field, but if you're
not suffering any of the standard concussion
symptoms, I suppose you have my go-ahead to
resume playing."

Mom gives me one more hand squeeze,
and we stand up together. *Wow*, I think. *That
was easy.*

"Of course," Dr. Lopez says, "before I sign
off on anything, I still need to run a series of
neuropsychological tests."

"Neuropsychological?" I ask.

"It just means on your brain," Dr. Lopez
says.

"Should we be concerned?" Mom says.

"I don't think so, Ms. Duncan. If your

daughter feels as good as she says she does, she should pass with flying colors." She looks at me with her head tilted to the side, and I wonder if she suspects I've been lying to her. "Ready, Alyssa?"

chapter 22

just need to sit in my tree. If I can do that, everything will be okay.

I can handle losing Rick. The more I think about it, the more I'm sure of that. He may look perfect, but it's been a long time since our relationship has been perfect. The guy has muscle to spare, but he doesn't seem to have any fingers. Why else would a boyfriend stop calling his girlfriend *the week after she has a concussion?*

So, yeah, if Rick and I are through, I'll be just fine.

As for playing goal, I'm pretty sure I can give that up too. Soccer has been my life as long as I can remember, but maybe it's time to try something else. Maybe I don't have a choice. It took less than fifteen minutes to fail the doctor's brain tests and another fifteen for her to finish lecturing me about honesty and safety. Luckily, Mom was on the other side of the room during the lecture. Otherwise, I think she might have squeezed my hand hard enough to break it.

I was sure she would have a meltdown in the car, but I was wrong. Surprisingly, she stayed pretty calm and asked why I lied about how I was doing. I said because I didn't want to worry her. I could tell by the way her eyes wobbled that this made her feel worse, but she managed not to cry. She asked me to make a deal with her. If she tried not to get so upset about things, would I promise not to lie about my health? I said yes. When we shook hands to seal the deal, her hand wasn't as

viselike as before.

She told me that she still wanted to come to my game, even though I wasn't going to be playing in it, but I told her it wasn't worth it.

"When, and if, I ever play again," I said, "I'd love to see you in the bleachers. But I'd really rather not ride the bench in front of you."

Mom said I was being silly. "*Of course* you'll play again," she says. But she agreed to stay away from the games for now.

Anyway, I'm not so sure she's right. What if I don't get to play again? What if Becca's even better than me by the time my head heals? Could I deal with a future without soccer?

I hope so. If Mom can keep her cool after finding out her daughter still has a profound brain injury, then I should be able to keep cool over losing my spot on the team.

If I *do* lose my spot, I have two options: acceptance or bitterness. And the first option seems way better than the second.

No matter how many times I tell Ruth

that I don't want to pick on Becca anymore, she keeps sending me texts with ideas for more missions, more ways to humiliate Becca Miller. Ruth may be an evil genius, but she has serious issues with letting go of her anger. I'd rather quit the team tonight than end up like that.

If I do quit, maybe Mom can stop working so hard. Maybe I can take her job at Big's Bar and Grill. Come to think of it, if I become a waitress, I might as well stop the beast. Something tells me beasts don't get very good tips.

So yeah—maybe I'll quit.

Or maybe I won't.

I still need to think on it before I come to any conclusions, which is why I need to get to my tree as soon as possible. I do all my best thinking there.

After the last bell, I go straight to my gym locker and change into my uniform. Today's game isn't until six o'clock, so it's not surprising that I'm the only one in the locker room. I put my bag over my shoulder and head outside.

As I cross the athletic parking lot, I can already see the leafy top of the yellow poplar tree. It'll be nice to get up there and sit on one of the branches for a while.

I walk along the track for a while and then cut through the field. My tree's looking more and more inviting. When I get to the base of its trunk, I set my bag down and close my eyes. The waves of wooziness have receded over the last few days, but it's better to be safe. With my eyes still closed, I grab for a branch. Above the rustle of leaves I hear something I'm not expecting. A human voice.

I open my eyes. You have to be kidding me.

Rick and Becca are sitting above me. I watch Rick's dangling feet as he scoots closer and closer to Becca, then puts his arm around her.

I'm too stunned to understand whatever Becca's saying. Or to say anything myself, for that matter. Or even to hang onto the tree.

I land awkwardly, first on a knee and then on my shoulder. The branch I'd been grabbing must have rustled, or maybe I grunted in pain when I hit the ground, because as I get up I

hear Rick's voice: "Hello? Is someone down there?"

Instead of answering him, I pick up my bag and run. It's the first time I've run in a week, and I feel light-headed right away. I stumble and fall, but I lurch back up and keep going as fast as I can.

I don't know where I'm headed, but I'm in a hurry to get there.

chapter 23

don't get very far. I have to sit down in the parking lot and wait for the dizziness to go away. When it does, I stagger the rest of the way back to the school. I'm not really thinking anymore. I'm just going wherever my feet take me, which turns out to be the girls' locker room. I sit on the bench in front of my locker and close my eyes. My skin feels clammy. My stomach is wobbling. It feels good to have my head dropped, my eyes sealed tight.

I don't know how long I sit like that, but it must be awhile, because when I open my eyes, I'm surrounded by my teammates. They're changing into their uniforms and lacing up their cleats.

"You okay, Alyssa?"

It's only now that I realize Juanita has her hand on my shoulder. I give the same response I've been giving for over a week: "Fine."

"We better get going then," she says. "Don't want to miss warm-ups."

I follow her toward the door.

"Alyssa!"

It's Madison Wong, one of our team's defenders.

"Yeah?"

"You forgot your bag," she says.

▦ ▦ ▦

"Duncan!"

"What, Coach?"

"Where's Becca off to now?"

I look over his shoulder at my tree. *Is*

she still sitting up there? I wonder. "Got me, Coach."

"Am I ever going to be able to count on that girl?"

Sure, I think. *You can count on her. You can count on her to take your entire life away from you.*

"Guess Erin will have to play goalie," Coach says, rubbing his buzz cut.

"I'll play, Coach." I'm not sure who's more surprised—Coach or me.

"You know I can't let you do that, Duncan."

"Doc cleared me to play yesterday," I tell him. I dig around my bag and come up with the letter Dr. Lopez gave me. What it says, of course, is that I *can't* play. But that's in between lots of official medical jargon, enough to fill up the entire page. Rather than taking the time to read it, maybe Coach will just glance and take my word for it.

But he doesn't. He grabs the letter from me and brings it close to his face. Crap. I'm screwed.

The buzzer sounds. Time to start warm-ups.

Coach must not have gotten to the part where Dr. Lopez says I can't play, because he says, "Well, why didn't you say so earlier, Duncan? You have a jersey?"

I hold the yellow jersey up from out of my bag.

"What are you waiting for? Get out there!"

As I trot out to the field, I ask myself a different question—not *What am I waiting for*, but *Why am I being so stupid? Why am I risking my life for a soccer game?* Immediately, my injured brain comes up with an answer: *Because she doesn't get to take everything.*

She can have my boyfriend or my starting goalie spot or my tree. But she can't have everything. I get to keep at least part of my life, no matter how dangerous keeping it might be.

chapter 24

Unlike Greenridge, the Yeopin County Muskrats are able to get the ball into our half of the field and keep it there. This means I have to follow the ball as it moves from foot to foot and side to side. By midway through the second half, I've been splashed by so many waves that my legs are locked in the crouched position. We're winning 1–0, but I've needed to make two lunging saves to keep it that way. If I have to make another, I don't

know if I'll be able to get up again.

I started the game by yelling as I usually do.

"Back up, Addie!"

"Faith! Watch your right side!"

But at this point yelling makes me dizzy. Just *watching* the game makes me dizzy. I have to squint to make the players look less blurry.

I'm so tired I wish I could close my eyes and go to sleep. Juanita finally pushes the ball into Yeopin Valley's half of the field, and I can quit concentrating so hard. I allow myself to let my heavy eyelids meet for just a moment.

I think it's only a moment, anyway, but it must be longer. Suddenly, Coach is yelling at me, "Duncan! Cut off her angle!"

I open my eyes and see a Muskrat charging at me. I'm too late to go after the ball, so I get ready to dive one way or the other. I feel like I'm thinking and moving in slow motion. *Which way is she gonna go? Left? Right?*

I guess left, but my legs don't lift me off the ground like I want them to. It's a good thing they don't, though, because she doesn't

kick the ball to the left or the right. She kicks it right at me.

I can't move my hands fast enough to catch the ball or even to knock it out of the way. I can't even move them fast enough to protect myself.

The ball collides with my face, and I finally get to go to sleep.

chapter 25

"Alyssa! Alyssa!"

This time the shouts aren't just from Coach. They're from everyone. My athletic trainer. My teammates. My mom.

"Open your eyes, Alyssa! Please, please open your eyes!"

I do. Briefly. Before falling asleep again, I hear my mother say, "An ambulance is on its way."

"Stay with us, Alyssa!"

Voices I don't recognize join the noise. I look around.

"That's it. Just stay with us, okay?"

I'm strapped down to something.

"You're doing great, Alyssa."

This voice sounds like my doctor, but I'm not sure what she means. As far as I can tell, I'm not doing anything at all.

"Alyssa, can you hear me?"

I definitely recognized that voice—even if it's whispered into my ear. I open my eyes and I'm face-to-face with Becca Miller. Her long, lustrous hair swings in and out of my line of sight. "What do *you* want?" I mutter.

As always, she's surprised by the anger in my voice.

"Nothing," she says. "I just wanted to see if you were okay."

Now that her hair's not in my face, I can look around. "Why am I in the hospital?" I ask.

"You were knocked out again," Becca explains. "The doctor says you're lucky your brain didn't swell up even more than it did."

"How long have I been unconscious?"

"According to your mom, you've been in and out for a couple hours."

"Where is she?" Based on the numbness of my hand, she must have just left.

"Getting another box of tissues from the nurse," Becca says. "She wouldn't leave the room until I promised to keep an eye on you."

"Gee, thanks," I say.

Becca winces at my sarcasm. "Do you hate me or something?"

"You make it pretty easy," I say. "You stole my boyfriend and my position on the soccer team. You even stole *my tree*."

"Me? I *stole* . . . ?" Becca's face puckers up. Even her confused face is cute. "Well, you can have all those things back. I never wanted them in the first place."

"Becca, I saw you. Up in the tree. With Rick."

"How was I supposed to know it was your tree? Who claims a tree?"

"And next you're going to say you didn't know Rick was my boyfriend."

"Of course I knew that. That's why I

pushed him away when he tried to make a move on me. Here I was trying to tell him why I was quitting as a goalie, and all he wanted to do was get his hands on me."

Suddenly I'm the one who's making the confused face. "You want to *quit* playing goalie?"

"I hate playing goalie almost as much as I hate Coach Berg." The words come out in an angry rush followed by a huge sigh. "No offense, but it's way more fun to score on someone than to get scored on."

"None taken," I say. "I'm quitting too."

"What? You can't. If you quit, then Coach will make me the goalie forever."

"The whole swollen brain thing doesn't give me much of a choice, does it?"

"Not for this season. But your mom said the doctor thinks you'll be ready for next season." Becca's so excited that every bit of her is moving. Her fingers are drumming against her thigh and she's rocking back and forth on her heels. "Tell me you're going to keep playing goalie, Alyssa. Please?"

"I'll think about it," I say, even though I don't need to think about it at all. If and when it becomes safe, I will definitely play again. I already feel myself transforming back into the beast that I am. "You pushed Rick?" I ask.

"Right off the branch."

"Is he okay?"

"Um. Not really? He broke his arm. But the doctor says it'll heal in plenty of time for his season in the fall."

I know it shouldn't, but the image of Rick in a sling makes me smile. I guess he was right—the poplar tree really *is* dangerous. Especially if you try to hit on someone who's not your girlfriend.

Honestly, I'm impressed. Maybe Becca does have a little beast in her after all.

chapter 26

t's been more than a month since my second concussion, and the wooziness waves are pretty rare these days. In any case, I'm in no rush to get back on the field. The season's over anyway. We made it to the quarterfinals of the state tournament before losing 1–0 in overtime. Becca played great, but as soon as the game was over she told Coach she was never going to be a goalie again. He yelled at her, but what else is new? A part of

me was even jealous of her in that moment. If Coach is yelling at you, that means he's noticing you. Hopefully, next year he'll have a few reasons to yell at *me*.

Of course, I plan on doing plenty of yelling too.

But that's all a long ways away. The doctor explained that healing is a slow process full of little steps, and I've been doing my best to follow her advice. Still, I've decided to take a slightly bigger step than normal.

I've decided to climb my tree. In fact, I'm standing under it now. The leaves are still green, and they'll stay that way for the rest of the summer. I take a deep breath and grab a branch. After a few more breaths, I hoist myself up. Finding a comfortable spot, I look at the field and imagine my future.

about the author

PAUL HOBLIN HAS AN MFA IN
CREATIVE WRITING FROM THE
UNIVERSITY OF MINNESOTA.
HE LIVES IN SAINT PAUL,
MINNESOTA.

COUNTERATTACK

TWEEN FICTION H